From the same author:

Time to Kill
The Man from Blue Anchor
A Twist in the Tale (25 short stories)

Books for Children (From about 6 years to Young Adult)

Whiskers, Wings and Bushy Tails (Stories from Undermead)

There is a large collection of stories featuring the woodland inhabitants of the neighbourhood known as Undermead. There are birds, rodents, squirrels and other four-legged creatures, George (the little boy that lives in The Big House) and Bad Boy Badger and The Ooty Snooty Gang all living in, or close by, this lively woodland. There's even The Scarecrow that Ollie Owl, the wisest owl in the whole wide world, says is an inanimate object incapable of speech and there's the irrepressible Percy Pigeon, the world's worst poet!) Plenty of adventure, humour, loveable characters, moral lessons...and no unhappy endings!

Blackberry Bluff	Roland Rabbit
Good Deeds and Evil Intentions	Black as Night
Where is Woolly Woodmouse?	Links of Gold
Where is Dotty Dormouse?	SwaggerWagger
George and the Magic Jigsaw	Blackberry Pie
Three Wheels and a Bell	Rain! Rain! Rain!
Autumn (A Time of Magic)	Roland Rabbit
The Race	Curly Cat
Rebellion	Tap! Tap! Tap!
Quiz Night	

Stories you might like to read to children:

Granddad Remembers (But is he telling the truth?)

Millie Manx (The Tale of a Tail)

Ninky and Nurdle (Stories from Noodle-Land) *
ONE OF THE STORIES CAN BE VIEWED <u>for free</u> ON YOUTUBE /THE HOLE IN THE GROUND / TERENCE BRAVERMAN

All books are available from Amazon in paperback and many as eBooks.

Author link: amazon/author/Terence Braverman

Or click on this link:

https://www.amazon.co.uk/Terence-Braverman/e/B07H1C13KK%3Fref=dbs_a_mng_rwt_scns_share

Contact the author:

terry@terrybraverman.co.uk

www.noteablemusic.co.uk

Preface

This story is a work of fiction although the names of several characters and the titles of two plays ('M or N' and 'Murder on The Orient Express') were created by Agatha Christie. The Simplon Orient Express operated between Istanbul and Calais

Edward Ratchett is murdered by twelve people whilst travelling aboard The Orient Express. Amongst the twelve were a number of women. He was better known as in his home town of Chicago as Lanfranco Cassetti.

'M' and 'N' are pseudonyms given by British Intelligence to two German spies that operated in Britain during the Second World War. One of them is murdered.

Tommy and Tuppence Beresford are recruited to seek out the spies.

Two people, a man and a woman, each seek revenge.

Agatha Christie's role in this story is pure invention and a figment of my imagination!

STAGE FRIGHT

She was born on Christmas Day 191
5 and her parents had named her Holly. Holly, for
goodness sake! Why not Hollie?

Now, today, this minute, 1946, she was Sarah.

Her surname? Her surname was, and still is, Hollings. Holly
Hollings!

But now, today, this minute, she was Thompson. Sarah
Thompson.

"Sarah, this cannot continue. It's totally unacceptable."

"Suppose I disagree? Suppose I just go ahead?"

"There will be a price to pay," the tall gentleman replied.

"And if I refuse to pay it?"

"Do you not value your life above what you owe me?" the
man asked.

"I owe you nothing," Sarah sneered. "You're worth
nothing to me."

He was silent for several moments, appearing to evaluate her words, structuring an equation, formulating a calculation. If 'x' + 'y' = 'z' then...he shrugged.
Turning to her, he said,
"Your debt is cleared."
And shot her dead.

Or so the audience in *The Bournemouth Arts Theatre* believed until they remembered where they were and what they had been watching.
The curtains, which had closed as she'd fallen to the floor, swept open and Sarah Thompson appeared holding the hand of the tall gentleman. They bowed twice and then left the stage as the curtains swished together once more and they were hidden from those in the auditorium.
"Miss Hollings."
Holly turned and smiled as a stage hand called out her name.
"I have a message for you," he said as he withdrew an envelope containing a scrap of blue paper from the back pocket of his jeans.
"Thanks, Tim."
The writing was scratchy. Hastily written or written with difficulty.

It made little difference.

It was legible.

'I'm getting closer to you. LC'

It was cryptic message number one.

Agatha Christie looked up from her notebook and smiled when she recognised her visitor.

"Holly, it's lovely to see you again. How long has it been?"

"1973? You were working on a new book. I think you were going to call it Postern of Fate?"

"Ah, yes, I remember now. Well, I'm pleased to say that I completed it and it was published soon after."

The two women regarded each other quietly for several seconds.

Holly broke the silence.

"I've come to see if you can help me."

"Help you? You've always struck me as a competent problem-solver."

Holly sighed.

"The thing is...I believe I *do* have a problem but I don't know what it is!"

"My dear," Agatha said, "I'm not a mind-reader and neither can I call on Hercule Poirot. He's taking a holiday."

"Anywhere exciting?" Holly asked.

"Well, I haven't actually decided. How can I help you, my dear?"

Holly hesitated and then bent to one side to retrieve several sheets of pale blue notepaper from her handbag.

"***I know what you're up to***," Agatha read aloud.

This had been cryptic message number two.

"What exactly are you up to?" she asked.

Holly felt her cheeks redden.

"Nothing!"

"You told me when we last met that you were an actress. Have you upset a fellow thespian? Taken a role they'd hoped for, perhaps?"

Holly shrugged.

"The last time I was on stage I was shot dead. Does that count?"

Agatha smiled.

"Well, I do declare, you've made a remarkable recovery."

It was Hollie's turn to smile.

"Haven't I just?"

She passed another of the pages to Agatha who turned it over a couple of times before settling back to read it. This took barely a moment. There were just three words scrawled in large, irregular letters.

'*You killed Edward Ratchett.*'

It was cryptic message number three.

"I presume you played the part of Caroline Hubbard in a stage production of '*Murder on the Orient Express*'."

"As a matter of fact, I did. As another matter of fact, we *all* murdered Edward Ratchett."

"Yes, I know. I wrote the book."

Agatha frowned.

"First thing tomorrow, I'll phone a literary acquaintance of mine at *The Times.* See what light he can throw on Lanfranco Cassetti."

"Lanfranco...*who*?" Holly said.

"Lanfranco Cassetti. That's Edward Ratchett's *real* name."

Holly thanked Agatha for her time, left contact details and returned to her flat in Bournemouth.

"I would like us to put on another Agatha Christie mystery."

David Wisbech was trusted by *The Bournemouth Arts Theatre* to make good decisions based on his knowledge of its members, their weaknesses, their strengths and their availability.

"I've chosen the one about a spy investigation - '*N or M*' - and I reckon the role of Tommy Beresford would be splendid for our Dunc."

Duncan Morgan looked up, frowned and said, "I've no idea who Tommy Beresford is."

"*I* recognise the name."

David Wisbech looked into a pair of earnest blue eyes.

"He's the husband of Tuppence Beresford. The pair of them worked for British Intelligence during the Second World War. I saw the play in London a year or two back." David beamed.

"Excellent!" he exclaimed. "That's just perfect because I'd like you to play the part of Tuppence. You and Duncan should make an excellent pair of spies."

Holly felt exhilarated for the remainder of the morning. *The Bournemouth Arts Theatre* was an extremely popular and well-supported venue that provided her with regular work and a regular income.

The feeling of exuberance, however, evaporated as the day progressed and she recollected the visit to her friend, Agatha Christie. By mid-afternoon, when she finally set off home, her spirits were low.

Those strange, threatening notes were unnerving.

She turned the key in the lock to her flat, opened the door and stooped to gather up the morning's post.

The junk mail went straight into the scrap paper recycling bag. The credit card statement would be paid at a nearby bank next day. The blue envelope intrigued her. She didn't recognise the handwriting and the postmark was illegible. Holly wriggled a finger under the flap and along its length and withdrew a sheet of pale blue paper. She turned it over.

'You won't have to wait much longer. I'm coming to get you.'

There was no signature. Simply the initials *'LC'.*

The rehearsals were going well.

The play would go ahead in three weeks' time as planned.

The moment would arrive.

The players would try to calm their nerves and then take up their positions on stage. The warning bell would sound and three minutes later the curtains would sweep aside to reveal a loyal audience that eagerly awaited each production.

Duncan Morgan knew something was troubling Holly. The cast was holding one of its final dress rehearsals and she was fluffing her lines and stumbling over words that had presented no problem the previous week.

He regarded her closely as he acted out his role as Tommy Beresford.

"Well, you've been at San Souci longer than I have. Can you honestly say you think any of these people who were there last night could be a dangerous enemy agent?"
Holly looked blank for a moment.
"It ...it does seem a little...er...a little incredible..."
There was a longish silence and Holly shook her head.
Duncan mouthed the words *'there's the young man...'*
"There's the young man, of course," Tuppence Beresford said.
"Carl Von Deinim. The police check up on refugees, don't they?"

Fortunately, the rehearsal was nearing its end and Holly was spared further embarrassment.
As the cast wandered back to their dressing rooms, Duncan quickened his step, caught up with Holly, and placed a hand on her shoulder.
"Something's troubling you, Holly. Would you like to talk about it?"
Holly hesitated before smiling wanly and shrugging her shoulders.
"Thanks, Dunc, but I'm fine. Just a bit of bad news. Nothing too serious" and she hurried away.

*

It was at around 8.30 that same evening when the phone rang in Holly Hollings' flat.

Holly hurried towards the phone but stopped and hesitated.

'You killed Edward Ratchett.'

Those words were preying on her mind as was a recollection of the menace contained in the two previous notes and the letter she had received.

He knows where I live!

She was reluctant to answer the insistent jangle but when she finally reached out to raise the receiver the ringing ceased.

The sudden silence seemed to bounce off the walls.

Holly jumped involuntarily as her phone began ringing again.

"Holly Hollings," she said.

"Ah, thank goodness you're there. I thought you might be at a late rehearsal...or dead."

Holly recognised the calm voice of Agatha Christie with its slight Devon accent.

"No. I've only just got in. It's been hard day."

"I can call you again tomorrow..."

"No! I could use a friendly ear right now."
After a short silence, Holly continued.
"I fluffed my lines at rehearsals today," and she explained how her mind had been disturbed by the words written on the blue sheet of paper inside the envelope she had torn open.

'You won't have to wait much longer. I'm coming to get you.'

"Those words certainly don't appear in the novel as **I** wrote it!" Agatha laughed but then quickly apologised.
"Is there any clue as to who sent it to you?"
"No name. Just initials but they mean nothing to me."
"Tell me what they are," Agatha suggested.
"LC".
"Hm, that's interesting. Has your rep company ever staged "Murder on the Orient Express?"
"Yes, I believe so but not whilst I've been a member. Why do you ask?"

"Well…one of the characters in my original novel which, incidentally, is based on a true real-life murder, had the name Edward Ratchett."

Agatha could hear Holly sigh.

"But that was a pseudonym. His real name was Lanfranco Cassetti."

A moment's pause and Agatha added,

"**LC**."

"That's a coincidence," Holly said. "What's the relevance?"

"Remember I said I would call my literary friend at *The Times*? Well, that's just what I did…and guess what?"

"I've no idea," Holly replied.

"Well, my friend shares a close relationship with an officer at Scotland Yard. He tells me that not only was Edward Ratchett murdered on that infamous train…it appears that three thespians playing female roles in productions around Britain have also died recently in somewhat mysterious circumstances!"

*

Time slowed as Holly's mind tried to absorb what Agatha had just told her.

"You've gone very quiet. Are you okay, dear?"

"Er…yes, well, no, not really. I still don't understand. Are you warning me to avoid a role in *'Murder on the Orient Express'*?"

"It's a bit more complicated than that, I'm afraid."

Holly could **hear** her heart thumping.

"What do you mean? What are you saying?"

"My friend at *The Times* has heard of further unexplained and, as yet, unsolved deaths."

"Are you telling me that **more** actors have died after appearing in *'Murder on the Orient Express'*?"

"No…but I feel I should warn you that two actresses **have** recently been found dead in their homes. On stage, they had both played a role that had them witness the murder of a character from one of my novels."

"Are you saying my life might be in danger?" Hollie asked hoarsely.

"Well, the thing is, my dear, both had played the role of Tuppence Beresford in *'N or M'*"

Hollie gasped. Her ears were ringing but Agatha hadn't quite finished.

"Tell me, dear. Which of my character's lines did you fluff today?"

David Wisbech listened open-mouthed as Holly explained why she would not be playing the role of Tuppence in '*N or M*'.

"Oh, come on, Holly," he pleaded, arms spread wide as she finally fell into an embarrassed silence.

"You've only the word of that woman."

"***That woman*** knows more about murder than Nero!"

David took a slow, deep breath.

"Get me some proof. Speak to her. Show me press cuttings."

"What...*now*?" Holly said.

"Not *now*, obviously. We have rehearsals to get on with."

Holly frowned.

"And you expect me to take part in them?" she asked incredulously.

"Of course...until you can show me evidence that might make me think differently."

*

"I'm so sorry to call you back so soon."

Holly tried to gauge Agatha's reaction. Friendship had its limits, did it not?

"My dear girl...you can call me whenever you like."

"Really?"

"Of course...but it doesn't mean I'll pick up the phone!"

Holly could hear Agatha chuckling to herself.

"As it happens, I've finished writing for today."

"Well, if you're sure..."

"I'm absolutely certain. If I tell you a secret will you promise to share it with everybody you meet?"

"I'm guessing it's a secret that might increase the sales of whatever it is you're presently writing?"

"You'd make an excellent assistant to Hercule-Poirot!" Agatha teased.

"Do you have a title?"

"Of course. It's at the top of page one!"

When Holly had stopped giggling, she added,

"I'm giving it a festive title. I'm calling it '*The Adventure of the Christmas Pudding*'".

"Any clues?"

"Hm...there's Poirot and there's an Egyptian prince..."

"And a Christmas pudding?" Holly suggested.

"I'm divulging nothing more other than to add that a valuable ruby is stolen over the Christmas period. Now, my dear, how can I help you?"

*

"When you spoke to me earlier you told me that...that **two** actresses had been murdered. Two actresses both of whom had played the part of Tuppence Beresford."

"You've a good memory, my dear. That's what makes you such a success in what you do on stage."

"Not right now I'm not! Right now I'm terrified."

"*Terrified*? Terrified of what, may I ask?"

"Going on stage."

"That's called stage fright. All players seem to suffer from it at one time or another."

"You don't understand," Holly stammered.

"I've just been handed the role of Tuppence Beresford in our next production!"

It could have been fifteen seconds before the conversation resumed.

Holly was first to speak.

"Please...can you tell me what you know about the

deaths?"

"The *murders*?"

"Yes, the..." Holly had difficulty adding the final word to her reply.

"I'll need to contact my literary friend again. Either that or see if my local library can dig up back-copies of *The Times*."

"Thank you. Thank you so much," Holly said before adding,

"I've told David I'm not prepared to play the part of Tuppence Beresford. Please tell me I've made the right decision."

Holly could sense Agatha using her nimble mind to rationalise arguments both for and against the decision she had made.

"If I was Hercule-Poirot," she said, "I think I would tell you to sacrifice the part. In fact, I think he would suggest giving up the entire production until sound evidence of safety is established."

"You **would**?" Holly gasped.

"**He** would," Agatha parried. "What **I** suggest is that you carry on with the play. Meanwhile, I will see what I can discover."

"But Hercule-Poirot disagrees with that decision!" Holly

exclaimed.

"Yes, my dear, but Hercule-Poirot doesn't always follow my advice."

Holly was forced to curb her impatience for the best part of a week. During that time she bowed to David's insistent demands and resumed rehearsing the lines of Tuppence Beresford in *'O and M'*.
She found herself regarding the other cast members in a ridiculously-suspicious light.

*

Five days later, towards the end of a day's rehearsal, there was a kerfuffle from the back of the hall. A bustling figure had pushed open an entrance door to the auditorium and stood for a moment behind the rows of empty theatre seats.

21

Although the entrance had been somewhat dramatic the appearance of the intruder was quite the opposite. Curls in her greying hair, pearl earrings and a pearl necklace, the smartly-dressed woman strode down the central aisle towards the stage.

"Excuse me," she said in a clear voice as she marched briskly towards David Wisbech.

"Excuse *me*!" he responded. "You can see we're rehearsing."

Holly was on stage with James Randall, a male member of the cast, and appeared confident delivering her lines.

Agatha recognised the words at once. They were from '*O and M*'.

James, in the role of Tommy, was locked in an exchange with his wife, Tuppence.

"*I have often noticed that being a devoted wife saps the intellect.*"

"*And where have you noticed that?*"

"*Not from you, Tuppence, Your devotion has never reached those lengths.*"

In her mind Agatha could hear an audience laughing. What Tuppence had to say in response might have rapidly brought their laughter to a halt.

*

"What on earth do you think you're doing, madam?"
David Wisbech was furious.

"Listen, my dear," Agatha said sweetly. "I have something
of importance to tell you."

"What on earth **of importance** could you possibly have to
tell me?"

He began to turn away.

"We have a rehearsal in progress. Or hadn't you noticed?"

"Oh, I certainly noticed," Agatha replied.

"If you want tips on acting you can speak to me later. If
you want tips on writing talk to Agatha Christie."

"My dear," Agatha said wistfully, "she talks to me all the
time. Sometimes I get quite fed up with the sound of her
voice!"

Whilst Agatha was incurring the displeasure of David Wisbech in Bournemouth, Dorset, Luigi Cassetti was wiping tears from his eyes in Chicago, Illinois.

He had loved his father as greatly as his enemies had loathed him. So be it. His father had told him 'always call in your debts'. He was about to do that.

*

It was December 1935, the month that his father had been the victim of a revenge murder aboard the *Simplon Orient Express* whilst travelling from Istanbul to Calais. Luigi shivered as December's icy wind whipped around the church. He began shuffling along a path covered in several inches of snow. The outdoor temperature had dropped below zero. It hadn't felt a great deal warmer inside the church where he had been honouring the memory of his father, Lanfranco, who had been stabbed to death in a revenge attack by twelve strangers each of whom had been wronged by him in the past.

Departing from LaSalle Street Station, Chicago, early next morning, his train travelled along the railroad's Water Level Route to Grand Central Terminal, New York City.

From there, a PanAm 'Flying Cloud' clipper completed his journey to London.

For Luigi, his father's murder, a two-way journey of revenge, had now become a three-stop journey of retribution.

David Wisbech had no choice other than to halt the rehearsal of '*N or M*'.

The cast, initially amused by the woman's forceful interruption, had continued delivering their lines. Her aggressive finger-wagging and disapproving frowns made them nervous, however, and after several minutes an edgy silence occupied the stage.

David glowered at Agatha, pointed to a set of wooden steps and indicated she should follow him. Once on the platform she was led 'stage left' to a cramped office-like room which served as the repertory company's administrative hub.

"So that makes five women in total that the police are

aware of! The person, or *persons,* carrying out these murders may have the intention of increasing this number. You should show a degree of regard towards the ladies in your company and give them immediate leave of absence."

"We can't do that! We'd have to close down!"

"There are alternative solutions," Agatha opined.

"My men are not dressing up as women!" David spluttered.

Agatha laughed.

"Shakespeare managed to write some rather famous plays without women playing the female roles," she retorted.

"That may well be so...in fact, that *is* so, but if there are female characters in your stories then I intend they be played by women. We are no longer living in the seventeenth century."

"Indeed, we are not," Agatha agreed, "but murder is timeless."

David admired the writer's natural wit and concern towards those chosen to enact roles in her stories. He suggested lunch to which Agatha readily agreed.

"How far have the police reached in this implausible piece of black theatre?" he asked over a somewhat sad-looking salad sandwich.

"I'm given to understand…not very," Agatha replied. "They **do** have some grainy fingerprints found on a victim's stockings but they don't match anything on their files."

"And is there a murder weapon involved?"

"Apparently so and it is linked to all the attacks."

David tapped his fingers impatiently on the table and waited whilst Agatha rummaged through a swollen handbag.

She held up an old black-and-white photograph daubed with tea-stains.

"I managed to obtain a copy of this several years ago," she said. "It's a photo of the actual knife used by the killers of Lanfranco Cassetti aboard the Orient Express."

"And how were the present-day victims…er…removed?"

"I couldn't discover any more than I've just told you. The whole business is hush-hush in order not to cause unnecessary alarm."

David's eyes opened wide in astonishment.

"That's hardly reassuring for those actors who have, or will be, working on stage adaptations of '*Murder on the Orient Express*'."

"The police say they will keep an eye on those identified as at risk," Agatha said before adding, "but I think that's highly unlikely. Now you know as much as I do."

"I doubt it," scowled David.

"Why do you say that?"

"Well, for one thing, I've not heard you make mention of my current production. What's the situation regarding *'O or M'*?"

Agatha had expected to be asked the question but had wanted to avoid answering it until strictly necessary. That moment had arrived.

"What has Holly told you?" she asked.

"Only as much as **you've** told her!" David exclaimed.

"Which is...what exactly?"

"That two actresses and three actors playing the roles of Tuppence and Tommy Beresford had recently been murdered."

Nothing more was said for several seconds as both regarded each other cautiously.

Agatha was first to break the silence.

"Look, I understand your reluctance to cancel *'O or M'* but the fact is...the police have no leads as to who might be responsible for these deaths. They cannot say with any certainty whether more than one person is involved."

"Oh, my god, it gets worse! If they've no idea who the killer, or killers, might be, how they possibly protect my actresses?"

Agatha nodded.

"They have been offered help from somebody with extensive background knowledge of the two individuals known as *O* and *M.*"

David raised his eyebrows.

"And are you able to name this person?"

"Oh, yes. In fact, you've already met her."

"Oh, no," David groaned. "Don't tell me it's…"

"That's right, David. It's me!"

If the weather was agreeable he would take an evening stroll along the promenade. England had become a second home to him and Bournemouth his chosen place of residence when in the country.

He bitterly resented the fact that he had never had the opportunity to meet his father, let alone discuss with him his wartime experiences exploiting weaknesses in Britain's security service.

The British had killed his father, whom they had given the code name *'N'*, had shot him dead and in doing so had saved the life of British agent Tuppence Beresford. And they had done it here, here in Bournemouth. It gave him a form of cruel satisfaction knowing that his father's female accomplice had escaped and returned safely to Germany. They had called her *'M'*.

His father had been a brave man, regarded as a hero by those few in Germany who knew of his clandestine activities in Britain. The British people knew him as Commander Haydock. British Intelligence simply referred to him as *'N'*.

These things he had learnt from his mother several years after the war was over. As he had grown older so his determination to avenge his father's death had increased. They were still killing his father in Britain.

British actors killed him each time they set foot on stage and portrayed the characters from Agatha Christie's book *'N or M'*.

He smiled to himself.

Well, there was a price to pay and three actors and two actresses had already paid that price in full.

His smile became grim.

He'd discovered that no more than a hundred yards away *another* theatre was producing yet *another* production of *'N or M'*.

So be it. The lure was irresistible.

"Are you suggesting that the identities of *'N'* and *'M'* are known to you?"

"David…" Agatha began, "if I knew that I'd have already informed the authorities."

David Wisbech grinned mischievously. It softened his features and Agatha thought it suited him far more than the forbidding countenance he normally adopted.

"I wish I could believe that!" he exclaimed.

"You *don't?*" Agatha asked.

"Not for a moment."

"So what *do* you believe?"

"I believe you intend to seek out the villains yourself." Agatha laughed.

"That's an unconvincing laugh if ever there was," David said. "You should consider acting as a career."

"I believe I'm better at writing words than remembering them."

"I intend that the play go ahead, you know," David said. "Despite your concerns, which I know are sincerely expressed, there are wages to be paid and expenses to be met."

"The cost may well be higher than you imagine," Agatha retorted. "I mean, what price do you put on somebody's life?"

"Anything else?" David asked. His patience was running thin.

"Yes, my dear," Agatha replied somewhat jauntily. "There is a second reason for my presence in Bournemouth. I need a holiday. A long holiday. I need to escape from my writing and the pressure it places both upon me and those who dare come near me."

"Oh, no!" David drew his hand to his forehead.

"Oh, *yes,* my dear. I've negotiated terms for an extended booking at *The Getaway Hotel* close to the promenade."

Rehearsals for the play would continue.The role of '*N*' had already been given to Duncan Morgan and, in the absence of Holly, who had followed Agatha's advice and withdrawn, the part of his accomplice '*M*' would go to stand-in Hilary Williams. She had been with *The Bournemouth Arts Theatre* for several years and could be relied upon to turn in a good rendering of the character. Hilary's diction was clear and refined and bore none of her mother's guttural characteristics.

Growing up in Cuxhaven, on Germany's western coast, an elderly retired teacher would visit six times a week to instruct her in the English language.

Her mother, Monika Baltz, spoke English fluently and without any trace of an accent. She required her daughter, Aneka, to have that ability, too.

Aneka knew that her mother had once spent several years in Britain. It was only recently, however, that she learnt when and why.

Monika Baltz explained how, during the Second World War, she had been a spy, known to British intelligence simply as *'M'*, and that her partner had been known as '*N*'. These were the code names given to two of Hitler's most dangerous agents.

She told her how Tommy and Tuppence Beresford had been recruited by British Intelligence to hunt them down. When they successfully confronted them, '*N*' threatened to kill Tuppence but before he could do so was himself killed by a British agent. His female accomplice *'M'* escaped amid the confusion and eventually found her way back to a coastal inlet close to her home in Cuxhaven. It was several years before Aneka Baltz was presented with a one-way ticket to London by which time she had become a well-spoken, sophisticated young lady. Her cultured British accent, a place at a leading drama school and the background influence of her mother, soon led to acting roles. At this point she changed her name to Hilary Williams, an unassuming choice, easily remembered, easily forgotten.

The first night's performance of 'N' or 'M' was going well and had reached a high-point in the drama.

The audience held its breath as Tuppence Beresford found herself trapped against a wall and confronted by Commander Haydock, the man known as 'N'.

The spy's arm was extended and in his hand he held a revolver. He lined-up Tuppence in its sights, a finger curled around the trigger, on the point of firing, when Tommy Beresford burst into the room, caught him by surprise, and brought the man down with a single shot.

'M' smiled grimly. She communicated neither shock nor panic. She rushed straight at Tommy, snatched the gun from his hand and pushed him aside. Pausing only to snatch a breath, she ran out through the open door and along a corridor. In the surprise and confusion that followed, she made good her escape. A waiting car had its door open and she leapt inside. The car sped away leaving behind her dead fellow-spy.

The audience applauded and waited for the curtains to close on the scene. Nervous anticipation was followed by a scream from a woman in the front row. Blood pooled across the stage in front of her and dripped on to the auditorium floor. At this point, the curtains *did* close. They closed on the lifeless body of Duncan Morgan, the first male actor to die in a stage production of *'N' or 'M'*.

The PanAm flight from New York City landed smoothly on the concrete runway at London airport.
The journey had been smooth, too, but Luigi felt tired and lightheaded.
Chicago in December had been bleak and cold and London felt only marginally warmer. He looked forward to settling into his hotel in Bournemouth and having a glass or two of rye.

He'd checked out Bournemouth on a map and in a travel guide. It would never have been a choice destination for him but it was a decision made out of necessity. It was in Bournemouth that a stage production based on a book by Agatha Christie had taken place last year. He was making a calculated guess that the cast lived in the vicinity although, in point of fact, there were just three cast members that merited his attention. All were female and all three had been instrumental in the murder of his father. They knew the man by his assumed name of Edward Ratchett. Edward Ratchett was Lanfranco Cassetti. Lanfranco Cassetti was his father.

He knew that bombs had fallen on the coastal town during the war.

His father, Lanfranco, had once told him so. That, of course, was before he was brutally murdered aboard *The Orient Express* by twelve strangers. Luigi gained no satisfaction from knowing that Lanfranco had made his mark in British folklore courtesy of a British writer named Agatha Christie.

He made a mental note of the road on which his seaside accommodation was situated. *The Getaway Hotel* sat alongside the Westover Road. He'd grab a cab to take him there.

Duncan Morgan, who had played the role of the German spy 'N', was dead, presumed murdered. The gun was found not to be a stage-prop replica containing harmless, booming blanks, but to be a serious weapon containing a single live round.
The guns had somehow been switched but by whom? And when? And why?

*

The theatre had been forced to close. The police insisted upon it.
An appeal for any information, however vague, had been broadcast on the local radio and television stations. Posters were displayed in shop windows. Nobody had come forward with any helpful information although a person claiming to be Agatha Christie's mentor and ghost

writer had made an anonymous phone call to the local police station. The caller had claimed responsibility for the murder and that he had another planned. The call had been traced to a phone cubicle beside the reception office of a psychiatric ward in a nearby hospital.

"Listen, my dear," Agatha said in a patient voice. "I **do** know what I'm talking about."
Her elbows had settled on the counter that had *'Enquiries'* written above it. The young police woman manning the desk eyed the elderly woman suspiciously.
"Really, madam? Three women whose lives are in great danger?"
"If you don't get a move on they will no longer be in danger because **they will be dead!**" The police officer looked alarmed. She pressed the buzzer-bell on the counter three times in rapid succession. A male colleague,

looking even younger than she did, opened a partition door and hurried through.

"Everything all right?" he asked glancing at both women.

"No, it certainly isn't, officer!" Agatha said fiercely.

The policeman gave his colleague a questioning look but she simply shrugged her shoulders.

"She just burst in and informed me, cool as you like, that three women are going to die."

The young man paused for a second or two before turning his attention to Agatha.

"Forgive me asking, madam, but have you had a glass or two of wine?"

"Don't be impertinent!" Agatha roared, any attempt at decorum put aside. "I am Agatha Christie!"

"Here, I've heard of you," the policeman said. "You're a famous artist, aren't you?"

"And you, young man, are probably a famous fool. Fetch Arthur Hambleton, please."

"Mister Hambleton?" spluttered the young man. "But he's the Chief Constable!"

"I know very well who he is," Agatha snapped.

*

Gillian Hemings was in nostalgic mood.

Could the best part of a year have passed since her appearance on stage in a production of '*Murder on the Orient Express*'? She recalled her role as the contentious Mrs Hubbard as though it was only yesterday...

'*Don't you agree the man must have entered my compartment to gain access to Mr. Ratchett?*'
...to which Princess Dragomiroff had tartly replied,
'*I can think of no other reason, madame.*'

Gillian smiled. The audience had laughed because Agatha Christie's script prevailed upon her to constantly interrupt other people's conversations and divert it to stories of her daughter.

Gillian Hemings stopped smiling when she recalled the gruesome scene in which she had taken her turn in stabbing that awful Ratchett man sitting smugly in an adjacent compartment on the train.

The retractable knife had been no more than a stage-prop but she had shuddered then just as she shuddered now.

*

The heavy front-door-knocker thumped twice and made her jump.

She rose to her feet supported by shaky legs and opened the door slightly, peering through the narrow gap.

Two figures stood either side of her doorstep.

One wore the uniform of a police officer and the other was a smartly-dressed elderly woman.

"May we come in, please? This shouldn't take more than a minute or two of your time."

Gillian paused, hesitated, and then stood aside beckoning them into her living room.

The smartly-dressed woman immediately spotted a framed photo on the wall above a mirror.

"I recognise **this** face!" she exclaimed. "It's Agatha Christie, I believe."

Gillian's face broke into a smile and she asked,

"Are you a fan? I adore her. Last year, I played a character from one of her novels."

"Mrs Hubbard, perhaps?" Agatha asked.

"Why, yes!" Gillian exclaimed. "Are you familiar with the story?"

"Only insofar as that I wrote her lines."

"You wrote…?" Gillian gasped and brought her hands to her mouth.

"It's you, isn't it?"

"That rather depends on who you think I am."

Gillian Hemings had been easy to locate. Her phone number and address were in a directory.

Deborah Coney-Smith was not listed and the police contacted the local authority who, in turn, consulted the local electoral register and eventually her address became known.

She lived on the edge of town in a large detached house. The property stood in a picturesque setting at the end of a longish drive.

Agatha Christie had the Chief Constable, Arthur Hambleton, as her companion on this, the second visit to an actress who had appeared last year in '*Murder on the Orient Express* '.

Arthur Hambleton has been intrigued by Agatha's conjecture that three actresses were in grave danger of death at the hands of an unknown killer.

He rang the bell and the ding-dong chimes brought a well-dressed, somewhat haughty woman to the door.

"Can I help you?" she asked and showed no surprise that a police officer and a plainly-dressed woman were standing before her.

It was Agatha that spoke first.

"Does the name Mary Debenham mean anything to you?" she asked.

Deborah Coney-Smith was taken aback. Her eyes opened wide.

"Who *are* you?"

"I'm somebody who knows Mary Debenham very well indeed. I have reason to believe that if you are familiar with the name...perhaps as an actress in a stage-play apropos a train journey..."

Agatha noticed the other woman trying to conceal a smile.

"You are Agatha Christie, I rather think,"

"I rather think I am," Agatha replied. "May we come in?"

Once all three were comfortably settled into easy chairs and coffee had been poured Arthur Hambleton opened the conversation.

"Unfortunately, I'm not able to enter into a full explanation of what I'm about to tell you."

He saw concern in Deborah's eyes.

"Has something happened to my Billy?" she said.

Arthur looked puzzled.

"Billy?"

"My dog. He went missing early this morning. I've had him for years. He's really quite old."

"Er, no. I'm not here about Billy."

At that moment there was a scuffling sound from behind the settee and the curly-haired head of a white poodle poked out.

"Another mystery solved," Agatha Christie chuckled.

*

"As I said, I cannot go into details, but we have reason to believe that actresses who have previously played roles in

'*Murder on The Orient Express*' are being targeted by...somebody."

"**Somebody**?" Deborah's eyes were full of concern.

The Chief Constable chose his words carefully.

"They had received letters containing a non-specific warning. I'm sorry. I can say no more than that. Have **you** received such a letter?"

"No," Deborah snapped as she stroked Billy's head and muttered '*naughty boy*' before adding "in what way...targeted?"

"The actresses had each been given the role of one of Ratchett's female murderers in '*Murder on the Orient Express*'."

"There must be dozens of actresses who've done so," Deborah said.

"Granted. But our enquiries have placed just three within a ten-mile radius of Bournemouth."

Agatha smiled encouragingly.

"You are the second of the three actresses we have located."

Arthur Hambleton stood up.

"Please take this threat seriously. Make sure your home is secure. Keep an eye open for anything out of the ordinary."

"I'm perfectly capable of looking after myself!" Deborah remonstrated."

Agatha's eyes twinkled.

"That's what Edward Ratchett thought."

*

Luigi Cassetti drew a deep breath and took another lungful of the fresh, evening air that was blowing gently along the promenade.

His evening had been uniquely eventful, particularly as the excitement he was normally accustomed to took place four thousand miles away from here back in Chicago.

His father had taught him well and it had become his legacy to take over running the family business. And it was an effective and profitable business, too. Who said crime didn't pay? It paid handsomely.

He hummed to himself as he speculated on the front page news story of tomorrow's local newspaper.

"You okay for our final visit of the evening?" Arthur Hambleton asked. "It's just that you look ready for a night's sleep."

"I wouldn't want to miss out on a visit to royalty," Agatha replied.

Arthur looked puzzled.

"Royalty?" he asked.

"Princess Dragomiroff, no less."

*

The Chief Constable knocked on the door of a terraced property in a less salubrious backstreet of Bournemouth. He knocked a second time when there was no response.

"Probably out," Agatha suggested. "It's a pleasant enough evening."

Arthur peered between half drawn curtains.

"Leaving on the lights and the television…and leaving the door unlocked?"

"Hello? Alison Ruskin?" he called out. "Police! Can we have a word, please?"

Agatha frowned and pushed the door open wider.

"Princess Dragomiroff. Are you home?"

There was no reply.

"Er...let's try this a little differently," Arthur suggested.

"Alison. I'm a Chief Constable of police. Could we have a word, please?"

The house remained silent.

Arthur shrugged and paced forward across a small living room covered in worn carpet and bordered by brown wooden skirting.

On the walls were several framed black and white photos. Agatha walked up to one of them and found herself staring at a beautiful young woman. She was finely dressed and wore a smile that lightened the dingy room.

"Princess Dragomiroff, I presume?" Arthur said as he peered over Agatha's shoulder.

Agatha laughed.

"I rather doubt it. Princess Dragomiroff was an ugly old lady with a yellow, toad-like face. This is Alison Ruskin, the actress."

"I hadn't realised the profession was so poorly paid," Arthur commented looking around the sparsely-furnished room.

"Gambling. Drink. Lavish lifestyle," Agatha half-muttered. She turned to face the Chief Inspector.

"You're far better off as old Mister Plod," she stated.
Then she gasped.
"Oh, my Goodness!" and she pointed to an old sofa positioned diagonally across a corner of the room.
There were three worn cushions distributed neatly along the seating area.
There was one wrinkled, blood-spattered old hand hanging over the top.
Attached to one finger of the hand by means of an adhesive strip of Elastoplast was a note.

'You had a hand in my father's murder. Was it this one?"

Investigators moved into the house and soon after an ambulance had taken away the body.
The homes of the two other actresses visited by Agatha and the Chief Constable were placed under twenty-four

hour surveillance.

*

Agatha had Arthur drive her to the promenade. She thanked him for the lift and said she would like to walk for a little while before returning to *The Getaway Hotel*.

She looked out at a calm sea silhouetted against a darkening sky. A few small boats bobbed gently up and down on the tranquil water. If only life was always this peaceful, she thought to herself.

If life was always this peaceful I wouldn't find anything to write about!

So deep in thought was she that she almost collided with a man ahead of her who was also enjoying the peaceful scene along the promenade.

"I'm so sorry," she said and stood to one side.

The man mumbled something unintelligible in response, crossed the highway and turned towards Westover Road. Agatha took a final glance out to sea, yawned, and then she, too, made her way to her hotel room in Westover Road.

After the car into which 'M' had leapt sped away from the theatre it left behind a scene of chaos. Another performer from 'N' or 'M' had been murdered.

The life of an actress playing Tuppence Beresford had been saved at the expense of the one lost by Duncan Morgan, performing the role of her husband, Tommy. Somebody had tampered with the gun. Somebody had substituted a stage-prop with the genuine article. Somebody had replaced a harmless blank round with one that was lethal and live.

The car slowed and merged with the predictable stream of holiday traffic. Just another car contributing to the town's summer congestion.

The woman began to relax. Before long she would finally leave Hilary Williams behind in Bournemouth and return to Cuxhaven, Germany, her mission successfully completed. She would renew her existence as Aneka Baltz, daughter of 'M', daughter of one of Hitler's most dangerous spies in wartime Britain.

"You're sure he'll be waiting?" Aneka Baltz asked.

"He's never let me down," replied the man driving the car.

Although the evening was growing dark, Aneka was just able to make out the black letters on a worn signpost as the car crept past.

'Hengistbury Head Beach ½ mile.'

"You've been adequately paid?" she asked Hans, the driver.

He nodded.

"And the boatman?"

"He'll be dealt with at the other end."

The car pulled into the side of the road.

Hans leaned to one side and withdrew a torch from the glovebox.

"I'll check he's waiting for us."

He clicked the torch on and off quickly three times.

From the area of the beach, a responding torch cast out two long beams of light.

He glanced towards Aneka.

"Everything's in place. Take this torch. You'll need to walk from here."

"You're not coming down to the beach with me?"

"You'll be fine. Just follow this path."

He pointed to the start of a sandy track and waited until she had taken her first tentative steps before turning his back on her and returning to the car.

He heard shuffling from behind.

He turned.

There was an explosion of light and sound.

The gun Aneka had snatched from the hand of Tommy Beresford when making good her escape from the theatre had been loaded with more than a single bullet. This one was lodged in the brain of her driver.

*

Aneka turned around and flashed the torch three times in the direction of the boatman. He was, no doubt, anxious to get going and wondering at her delay in joining him.

He was reassured by the flashing beams of light and then the soft sound of footsteps sinking into sand.

Shortly after, he made out her silhouette.

"This way," he whispered loudly enough for her to hear.

"No, *this* way," Aneka replied and her gun claimed its third life that night on Hengistbury Head Beach.

The boat continued to bob silently on the waves that were lapping the shore.

She returned to the car, found the key in the ignition, turned it and drove back towards the theatre before returning to an anonymous lodging house on the outskirts of Bournemouth.

Agatha was delighted to discover the bar in the hotel lounge was still open and serving tea. She looked around the room and spotted a small, circular table with two chairs. Placing her handbag on one of the seats she crossed the floor to the bar and ordered a pot of Darjeeling.

She was startled by the unexpected entrance of the man she had encountered earlier that evening on the promenade. He looked about him, got his bearings, nodded at her, and ordered half a pint of beer.

Agatha returned to her table and after about three minutes a young lady bearing a silver tray brought the tea and a small pack of finger-biscuits.

There were no stools at the bar and the man cast his eyes around the room looking for a place to sit. As his gaze alighted on Agatha, she raised a hand and beckoned to him.

"Would you care to join me?" she asked. "I'm just a harmless old woman who hasn't spoken to anybody this evening. I could use a little conversation."

She moved her handbag from the second chair and placed it on the floor beside her.

The man smiled, sat down and introduced himself.

"That's very kind of you, madam," he said. "My name is Luigi."

He saw no point in pretending. He couldn't possibly be known in this obscure little seaside town on the coast of Britain.

"And I'm Agatha. Are you staying long?"

*

Once their brief conversation had been concluded, Luigi returned to Room seven on the first floor.

He lay on the bed but couldn't sleep.

Thoughts and memories of his father, Lanfranc Cassetti, occupied his thoughts. He felt the pain no less now than he had all those years ago.

He knew his father was no angel. Angels did not abduct, ransom and then murder children. He knew his father had enemies. There were many. He had not become rich and successful on his chosen career path through kindness and compassion. The more ruthless he and his associates became, the greater the number of enemies he created. Enemies seeking revenge. Enemies travelling on *The Orient Express* that fateful December day in 1935 when the train had been brought to a standstill by an avalanche of snow across the track.

*

One down and two to go. He had targeted three actresses of repute. They had each been instrumental in the death of his father even though it was on stage. They had each raised the knife and dealt the blows that left him lifeless and bleeding. Revenge had been sweet for them but symbolic revenge and symbolic revenge was a room with that sweetness was now turning sour in Luigi's throat.

It had become the turn of Princess Dragomiroff to feel a sharp blade pierce her body. No matter that it was not the *real* Princess. He had no idea where *she* was. This was no space for subtlety.

He turned his attention to the second name on his list. Mary Debenham, Daisy Armstrong's governess, had been the architect behind the planning of his father's murder aboard *The Orient Express.* Cool and calculating, she was in for a surprise that even she could not have foreseen.

Revenge ***was*** sweet, he realised, and he was already savouring its taste.

Veronica Westlake felt she needed a holiday even though she had just returned from one. For two weeks she had walked the West Highland Way, stopping off on a sunny day beside the placid water of Loch Lomond, another close to Crianlarich and a third at a farmstead by open heather moorland close to Rannoch Moor.

She was exhausted. She was also due to start rehearsals for a new play in a couple of days' time.

Life was exhausting and a relaxing day followed by a Zopiclone-induced night's sleep amounted to a really good idea.

*

Agatha Christie thumbed through the reservations book of *The Getaway Hotel*. She had always been fascinated by people's names. They helped drive her imagination.
The hotel manager had agreed to her request once she had explained who she was and the substance of her curiosity.

The reservations book lay open on the reception counter. Agatha ran her index finger down the list of names, moving rapidly, sweeping over them without particular interest but then she suddenly frowned.
A name stood out. **'Luigi Cassetti'.**
The man at the bar the previous evening had introduced himself as 'Luigi'. That was interesting. What was more interesting, however, was his last name, *'Cassetti'.*

*

Luigi Cassetti stood several steps down from the top of the staircase and watched Agatha write something down in a notepad that she took from her handbag. The reservations book lay open.

"Agatha!" he called out as he descended. "Good morning."

Agatha looked up in surprise and closed the register.

"Oh!" she exclaimed. "Good morning…Luigi, I believe?"

The man smiled darkly and nodded. She could detect grimness beneath his geniality.

She desperately wanted to ask him questions regarding his last name but didn't want to appear too inquisitive or arouse any misgivings he might feel towards her.

Was he related to **Lanfranco** Cassetti, the man brutally murdered aboard *The Orient Express* in December 1935?

Veronica Westlake's plan was working as she had hoped. Roaming the town centre's shops at a leisurely pace, stopping for coffee and cake at a quiet café situated on a narrow side street and then slowly strolling home, relaxed in both mind and body.

She opened the front door.

Following a routine, she flicked the switch to the electric kettle and waited until the water was gurgling. She prepared a mug of tea. Too much coffee would not induce sleep. Opening a drawer beneath the kitchen worktop, she took out a packet of Zopiclone and popped two of the tablets into her mouth as she sipped her tea.

'Only take one of these when necessary' her doctor had advised. *'They can become addictive and less ineffective if taken regularly '.*

She lay on her bed with the cup of tea and picked up the script she had received for her next stage play. She would be travelling to a Bournemouth theatre once rehearsals were underway.

For the next twenty minutes she rehearsed her lines. She had reached Chapter Four.

'I don't mind lying in the least. To be quite honest I get a lot of artistic pleasure out of my lies. What gets me down are those moments when one forgets to lie -the times

when one is just oneself - and getting results that way that you couldn't have got any other.'

Veronica felt her eyes grow heavy. The Zopiclone was having its desired effect and she knew that sleep was close. Her interpretation of Tuppence Beresford's character in *'Murder on the Orient Express'* would have to wait until morning. Tomorrow was another day. There was always tomorrow. Wasn't there?

*

Luigi Cassetti spent several minutes standing by the back door just listening. He hadn't expected complete silence. The woman, Veronica Westlake, had entered the house ten minutes ago and the only sound he had heard since had come from behind the kitchen window at the rear of the house. A kettle that rattled as water reached boiling point. No radio. No television.

He stood back a little and looked up at the two bedroom windows. One was clearly visible, its curtains wide open. The other caused him to draw in his breath. The curtains on *that* window were being drawn shut.

The next morning, Arthur Hambleton drove to *The Getaway Hotel* to collect Agatha Christie. They had agreed to meet in the lobby at nine o'clock and then drive to the home of Veronica Westlake. Veronica had established a reputation within the acting profession by appearing in stage adaptations of Agatha's stories and *'Murder on the Orient* Express' in particular. She might be at risk.

When they reached her house they were met by the two police officers assigned to keeping an eye on the property. They confirmed that from their patrol car they had witnessed Veronica arrive home a little after six the previous evening. There had been no other callers and she hadn't been out since.

Arthur thanked them for the information and then rang the doorbell.

Nobody came to the door so he rang again.

There was no response. He rapped his knuckles against the glass panel set in the door and waited.

Meanwhile, Agatha had followed a gravelled path that ran round to the back of the house. There were two windows. One had its curtains open but the other had them drawn. She noted the unlocked back gate to the garden. It was swinging gently in the light breeze, opening and closing, softly hitting its latch. Behind it there was a communal passage serving half a dozen houses. So, she thought, this is how he gained access to the back garden unseen.

There was a wooden shed, too. It faced the bedrooms. Agatha tugged on its door and discovered it to be unlocked. It groaned creakily on rusty hinges as she opened it and sneaked a look inside.

Directly ahead of her, retracted and propped against a wall, stood a three-section lightweight aluminium ladder. She glanced down and noticed scrape marks on the wooden flooring. They formed a muddy track from the base of the ladder, across the threshold of the shed's door and onto the back lawn.

Two parallel furrows, a ladder's width apart, had compressed the grass. The tracks were recent, the grass still struggling to recover a vertical position.

The ends of the twin tracks had created holes where they had sunk into the gravel path beneath the bedroom window.

Agatha noticed small shards of glass lying amongst the shingle. She looked up.

The curtains were billowing gently in the soft breeze because there was little to prevent them doing so. The window had been smashed.

Agatha hurried back to the front of the house and told Arthur what she had seen. He returned to his car and made a phone call. Within five minutes a police van rounded the corner and as it drew up two officers leapt out. One of them opened the rear doors and a third man climbed down carrying an iron crowbar.

Arthur rang the doorbell again. It would be embarrassing if he discovered that Veronica was simply asleep and that he and his team were held responsible for damaging the door.

However, there *was* no response.

He beckoned forward the officer with the crowbar. Within thirty seconds the lock parted from the door leaving behind a damaged mechanism and a splintered frame.

Arthur remained outside with Agatha to examine the

tracks and broken glass she had discovered while the three police officers ascended the staircase leading up from the lobby.

A short time after, one of them leaned out of the smashed bedroom window and shouted down to the Chief Constable.

"She's dead, sir!"

'You're life's worth nothing let alone Tuppence. LC'
The note was attached to the end of a slim, six-inch knife. Five inches of the blade were buried in the heart of Veronica Westlake.

*

David Wisbech, director of *The Bournemouth Arts Theatre,* was slouched despondently in his chair. Opposite him sat the Chief Constable, Arthur Hambleton. Agatha Christie mooched unhurriedly behind him and enthusiastically examined the framed photographs dotted about the walls.

"That's me!" she suddenly cried out. "I was a *lot* younger then, of course."

She turned around.

"Holly said she'd be just a few minutes late. Her cat needed feeding."

Arthur smiled. David frowned.

There were two sharp raps on the door and David half-heartedly shouted, "Come in!"

Holly looked uncomfortable.

She had told David she was not prepared to continue in the role of Tuppence Beresford in *'N' or 'M'*. Others had died doing just that.

As it was, the theatre had been forced to close on the insistence of the local police following the death on stage of Duncan Morgan, the actor who had been playing the role of the German spy *'O'* and the sudden disappearance of Hilary Williams, the actress who had played his partner *'M'*.

"You're not in any trouble, my dear," Agatha said soothingly having noted Holly's discomfiture.

Arthur Hambleton smiled at her.

"Please take a seat, Miss Hollings. We have something to

discuss with you and your assistance could be of enormous help to us."

Holly could not imagine how she could possibly help the police with *anything.* She gave a small shrug of her shoulders and sat down.

*

"How would you feel about reprising your role as '*M*' if the theatre reopened?" Agatha asked.

Holly gasped and then turned her gaze towards David Wisbech.

"It would allow the theatre to reopen," he said gruffly by way of explanation.

"Miss Hollings, we're working on a plan," Arthur Hambleton began.

He paused.

"I must point out, though, that you could find yourself in a degree of danger."

"He's saying somebody might try to murder you, my dear, but it's nothing to worry about," Agatha said.

"Nothing to worry about?" Holly was practically shouting. "Since when has murdering me been nothing to worry about?"

"The Chief Constable will explain." Agatha tried hard to keep a straight face. She failed.
"I'm sorry, my dear. I apologise. This is not the right time for me to engage in flippancy."

Hilary was furious.
David Wisbech had contacted her. He had explained that the theatre was to reopen and preparation for "*N or M*" to recommence. He had said that Holly would be taking up her former role as '*M*' and that there was a particular reason for his decision. He refused to elaborate. However, he did reassurance Hilary that she would be offered a starring role in his next production.

Posters appeared in shop windows, advertisements in the local papers, interviews on radio and local television...

publicity, publicity, publicity.
Agatha Christie had a plan.

The plan offered a long-odds opportunity to catch a murderer and would be played out on the stage of *The Bournemouth Arts Theatre.*
Agatha Christie had found it difficult to convince David Wisbech and Arthur Hambleton of its merit but they eventually succumbed to her persuasive argument. She was, after all, in many ways closer to criminal intrigue than most. In fact, she **created** the intrigue.

*

'The Bournemouth Arts Theatre is pleased to announce that it will be reopening shortly with a play based on a classic novel by Agatha Christie. We look forward to welcoming you to a new production of 'O' or 'M' featuring Holly Hollings and produced by David Wisbech. Advance booking advised...'

*

Luigi Cassetti couldn't believe his luck.

He had returned to his room at *The Getaway Hotel* after a morning spent browsing a few shops followed by a bracing walk in a chilly wind along the promenade.

He put the leaflet on the sideboard. Somebody standing outside a Tesco store had shoved it at him and mumbled something about an advanced bookings office being open.

The leaflet contained information that persuaded him that another two or three weeks at *The Getaway Hotel* was worth the insignificant cost.

Several of the actresses that had appeared in *'Murder on The Orient Express'* were to take part in a rescheduled production of *'M' or 'N'*.

The actress that interested him most was Holly Hollings. Holly had previously played the role of Caroline Hubbard in *'Murder on the Orient Express'* and Caroline Hubbard had been one of the twelve passengers aboard the train on that fateful day in November 1935. Caroline Hubbard had been one of the twelve passengers that had stabbed his father to death. Now it would be the turn of Caroline Hubbard to die...or, in this case, Holly Hollings.

*

Luigi was in no hurry to return to Chicago. There was nothing waiting for him there other than the usual problems that needed to be dealt with.

As his father, Lanfranco, had often told him, *'Crime pays but when it doesn't pay well enough somebody's head might need a good shake.'* Sometimes a head needed shaking so hard that it fell right off.

The following morning, he intended to purchase a front-row ticket for the play.

*

Holly Hollings had the starring role of Tuppence Beresford once again and Hilary Williams would resume playing the character of the dangerous spy *'M'*. The gun used to shoot *'N'* would be supplied and inspected personally by Arthur Hambleton and David Wisbech before it ever came near the stage.

*

Arthur Hambleton and Agatha Christie had discussed their proposed plan at length. It required the murderer, or murderers, of actors and actresses from *'Murder on the*

Orient Express' and from *'M' or 'N'* to strike one more time.
It reminded Agatha of *'The Mousetrap'*.
The trap was set but would the mouse bite?

*

Aneka Baltz, *aka* Hilary Williams, had a plan, too.
She had successfully secured the role of *'M'* after Holly had followed Agatha's advice and stepped down. That had given her the opportunity to exchange the stage-gun for the authentic article. Duncan Morgan had died as a consequence and this was partial redress for the death of her mother's fellow-spy *'N'*.

It was beginning to grow dark as Holly left the theatre to return home.
"Would you like to invite me to walk home with you?"
Holly glanced up. Agatha had appeared at her side.

Holly smiled warmly and nodded.

"I could use a decent cup of tea," Agatha added, "and there's none more decent than yours."

"I thought the rehearsal went well today," Holly said. "I quite enjoy playing Tuppence Beresford."

Agatha looked thoughtful.

"And Hilary has the role of '*M*' so she's happy to have a major role, too."

"Yes," Holly said. "I'm pleased for her. I thought she might throw a tantrum when I was asked to take back my part."

"Nevertheless, it *is* unfortunate that it took the murder of Duncan for that to happen."

"Yes," Holly whispered softly by way of reply.

*

Hilary Williams kept to the shadows, never too close to be spotted, never too distant to lose sight of her quarry. She had dipped her toes in the English Channel and walked back up the sandy beach on to the promenade. The house had been easy to enter. Her skills had been honed by the finest instructors that wartime Germany could offer.

Gas from the unlit oven in the kitchen would be creeping steadily through the rooms. A match to a kettle or a pan of milk on a hob would create an explosion that would wreak death and destruction.
David Wisbech would need another Tuppence.
Just how many Tuppences could he afford to lose?
This could prove to be an exceedingly expensive production by the time she had avenged her mother's enemies.

"I've an idea!" Agatha exclaimed.
"You certainly have more of those than most of us," Holly responded.
"Let's have a drink and a bun at my hotel," Agatha said, taking hold of Holly's arm. "You've worked hard at rehearsals today. I want to see you relax for once. Call it an old lady's treat."
"I'm not used to hotels," Holly said. "Do I have to curtsy at the door?"

"Oh, you certainly do, my dear!"

"Damn!" Hilary Williams swore quietly to herself.
They weren't going straight back to Holly's house as she
had wrongly assumed.
She watched as they turned into Westover Road.
She wondered...could it really be?
The Getaway Hotel was her temporary lodging house with
twelve whole months booked. The cost was of no
consideration. Monica Baltz, her mother, had been richly
rewarded by the German authorities for her spying
activities and she had been generous to her daughter.

*

Agatha beckoned Holly forward. Holly giggled, curtsied,
opened the door and entered the hotel.
Hilary swore again, turned back towards the town centre

and ordered a sandwich and coffee at the first café she
found.

*

Luigi Cassetti needed to control his impatience. The play
was billed to open in three weeks' time. He would
be there on the opening night.

"May I walk home with you?"
Holly looked at Agatha quizzically.
"I'll be fine," she replied. "I'm a big girl now."
"It's such a lovely evening, though, and I could use some
fresh air."
Before Holly had time to protest a voice called out.
"Good evening, Mrs Christie."
Agatha turned round to see who it was.
"Mister Cassetti!" she exclaimed.
Turning to Holly, she said,

"Holly, this is an American gentleman I almost bumped into the other day. He's exploring our wonderful country."

"Holly...?" Luigi creased his brow. "I believe I came across the name *'Holly'* on a poster this morning. Something to do with a new play in town."

Holly beamed. "That's me! I'm Holly Hollings. I'm in *'M or N'*. It opens quite soon. Are you going to it?"

Luigi smiled broadly.

"Having now had the privilege of meeting its star in person, I most certainly am."

Agatha had insisted on walking back to Holly's home with her.

She had reiterated her desire to take in the fresh air but wasn't being totally honest.

The real reason for accompanying Hollie was a deep-rooted suspicion that something was amiss. She attributed it to her writing. Crime novels threw up the most extraordinary twists and turns.

As they approached her front door, Holly turned to Agatha.

"I'm definitely ready for bed but I'd love it if you could take a quick peek at my costume for the play. I've brought it home to turn up a hem."

"Yes, of course, my dear."

Holly turned the key in the lock and beckoned to Agatha.

"After you," she said before adding, "No need to curtsy."

Agatha smiled and stepped into the hallway. And stopped.

"Holly...have you been on the beach today?"

"You're joking! I've been too busy rehearsing."

"Bear with me," Agatha persisted, "but when did you last clean your hallway."

Holly gave her a strange look.

"Nothing personal, my dear. Trust me."

"This morning. Before I left for the theatre. I swept the floor."

"Did you have breakfast or a cup of tea before leaving the house?"

"I didn't have time. I was running a bit late."

"In that case, stay where you are. ***Do not enter***!"

Agatha backed out of the door and grasped Holly's arm.

Holly was thoroughly disconcerted.

"What is it? What's the matter? You're frightening me!"

Agatha grasped Holly's arm more firmly and answered,

"At least two things are the matter, my dear. There is sand on the hallway carpet and I believe I detected a faint smell of gas."

Aneka Baltz, known to her colleagues as Hilary Williams, sat in the lounge of *The Getaway Hotel.* The hotel was no great distance from Holly Hollings' house. She wondered if the noise of the explosion would reach this far.

She bore no personal grudge towards Holly. It was what she *represented*...a woman who might so easily have been responsible for the death of her mother, Monika Baltz, had she not escaped the clutches of MI5 after her fellow-spy had been shot dead.

Actually, Holly seemed a pleasant young woman and an accomplished actress.

She'd seen her at the hotel in the company of Mrs Christie, a prominent author, apparently. The two of them were chatting to the American gentleman of Italian appearance. It was something of a coincidence that the three of them were semi-resident at the same hotel and at the same time.

Aneka had made it her mission to take at least one more

life before returning to Cuxhaven, Germany.

It was a shame that Holly would shortly be blown to pieces.

There were times when life just wasn't fair.

*

The presence of police cars and a large van marked '**Royal Logistic Corps'** and '**Bomb Disposal'** outside Holly's home caused a degree of nervous excitement amongst her neighbours.

Houses either side had been evacuated and a cordon set up.

Someone speculated that she was a terrorist pretending to be an actress to cover up her shocking activities.

Another man assured his companions that he'd seen her wearing various disguises in a grocery shop nearby.

Another thought he had seen a light on in her shed late at night.

"Probably making a bomb then," he suggested knowingly.

"Don't be ridiculous. It's a gas leak. I can smell it!" said a man in a flat cap.

A police constable heard the conversations and ushered them further away from Holly's house.

"Please stand well back behind the barriers. There's a gas leak. There could be an explosion."

"There! I told you," said the man with the flat cap.

"I insist you spend the night with me at the hotel," Agatha said.

"You can return once the house has been declared safe and the investigators have gone about their business."

"Do...do you think it was deliberate?" Holly stuttered.

"Why would somebody want to...to hurt me?"

"**Hurt** you?"

Agatha sighed. "Whoever it is wanted to do more than hurt you. They wanted to kill you!"

Holly agreed to Agatha's proposal that she sleep on the settee in her hotel room that night. However, she insisted that the electric light remained on.

"But why would anyone want to hurt me?" she asked over

a cup of tea in the lounge.

Agatha shrugged.

"I can't be certain but I'm forming some ideas," she replied.

"If it's any consolation," she added, "I do not believe this to be a personal attack on you, *per se,* but on particular **characters** from the pages of some of my books."

Holly looked up as a figure approached their table.

Agatha pulled her lips together tightly.

"We have a visitor," she muttered beneath her breath.

"Ah, we meet again!" exclaimed Hilary Williams.

She gave Holly a prolonged stare.

"There's some kind of commotion going on not far from here," she said. "Police and all."

"Well, I can't imagine what it could me, my dear," Agatha responded, "this being such a quiet town quite devoid of any excitement."

Holly remained silent but Agatha continued,

"Did you go anywhere nice after today's rehearsals?" she asked. "The promenade and the beach are quite popular early evening."

Hilary hesitated.

"The promenade...yes, very pleasant but the beach...definitely not. I can't stand sand in my shoes."

Agatha glanced down surreptitiously and observed the clean, casual shoes on Hilary's feet. Hilary gazed openly at her footwear and smiled.

"Certainly not in these shoes," she said. "They're new. I bought them only today."

David Wisbech, Director of *The Bournemouth Arts Theatre,* felt as an amateur might on his first appearance on stage and yet this was simply a practice run. Arthur Hambleton, the Chief Constable, had been very persuasive.

"Nobody knows the actors and actresses better than you, David," he had said.

"And nobody knows **criminals** better than you*,"* David had replied, "but I wouldn't ask you to **be** one!"

David turned to face the empty auditorium. Every seat but one was upturned. The single one that **was** occupied accommodated Agatha.

"Can you see me?" she called out.

"You're quite conspicuous," David replied.

"Good. I'm in seat…" she looked at the metal plate, "thirteen, row B. He will be sitting directly in front of me. That is, seat thirteen, row A."

"He'll have you breathing down his neck," David observed.

"Unless I have **my hands** around his neck, of course".

"Of course, Agatha. That goes without saying."

"Then don't say it. Waste of words."

"Sorry. Just a bit nervous, that's all. I'm beginning to feel I'm actually **in** the play and that I've forgotten my lines."

"You do not **have** any lines. But you **do** have two eyes, fortunately, and we will need you to use both of them."

"Nevertheless, how can I be sure that the man sitting in front of you **is** the man you described to me?"

"He's of Italian appearance as you'd expect of a boy born in Italy growing up with an Italian father. Brown, wavy hair and eyes. Lightish skin. Roman nose…."

85

Hilary Williams, aka Aneka Baltz, wondered why David Wisbech was standing on the stage alone and talking loudly to a lone figure seated in the front stalls.

"How irritating," she thought to herself.

She had arrived at the theatre almost two before the scheduled performance expecting to have the place to herself.

The lighting, the props and the sound system had been tested, arranged and prepared the previous evening.

Aneka permitted herself a rare smile as she recalled her recent achievements in England. Her mother would be so proud of her. The smile quickly faded, however, as her thoughts returned to the present.

She slid silently and unseen into the crossover behind the closed curtains and slipped into the alcove where the smaller stage-props were stored.

*

After murdering the driver of the getaway car and the skipper of the small boat she had returned to the theatre where she had returned the gun to its shelf in the alcove. She had removed the remaining live rounds and replaced them with blanks.

She now observed that policeman, Arthur somebody, in the alcove examining the gun. He gestured to David Wisbech, who was centre stage, and gave him a thumbs-up. She took this to be the 'all clear' for the play to go ahead without human blood spilling all over the stage. Human blood was so difficult to clean off wood.

The Getaway Hotel on Westover Road was attracting a great deal of attention. Both the local *Bournemouth News* and the national press had been attempting to unravel the grim series of events at *The Bournemouth* Arts *Theatre*. When *The Sun* had discovered that Agatha Christie, no less, had a suite at the hotel, they sent a reporter and photographer down to Bournemouth to cover the story. Another newspaper revealed that Hilary Williams had been tracked down to the same hotel and speculated on whether the two were creating a twist in the plot to boost ticket sales of '*N or M*'. When '*an anonymous source*' revealed that Holly Hollings, the intended victim of a gas-filled house explosion, had been seen sitting in the lounge with Agatha, the conjecture only increased.

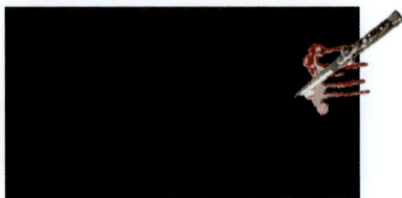

Luigi read the newspaper articles with amusement. They diverted attention away from his own, personal vendetta against those who had appeared in '*Murder on the Orient Express*'.
The play was as close as he ever would come to the actual killers of his father aboard that train.

Luigi caressed the slim weapon that had slid so easily into the inside pocket of his jacket. The short dagger with its tapering blade was identical in appearance to the one the travellers aboard that train had used to murder his father. In his skilful hands the stiletto would very soon embed itself deep within the heart of one of them.

'What a lark' she thought an Englishman might say as she slipped unseen into the alcove after the policeman had walked off.

Aneka removed the loaded gun from her jacket pocket and carefully wiped it clean of any fingerprints.

She had replaced the spent cartridges with live rounds after the beach killings.

She picked up the harmless stage-prop from its shelf in the alcove and slipped it into her pocket.

Should she be caught and searched no more than a harmless weapon would be discovered about her person.

When '*N*' was shot dead in tonight's performance of the play it would be for real just as it had been for Duncan Morgan.

Duncan had not been her favourite member of the theatrical group. She found him to have an exaggerated perception of his stagecraft. He had shown no interest in her either despite her playful, amorous advances.

However, his loss, his **total** loss to the theatre, was nothing compared to that of her next victim.

*

David Wisbech was the *long-time* director of *The Bournemouth Arts Theatre* with only a *short-time* to live.
He was also the man who had given her role of '*M'* to Holly Hollings.
This would be the last night of his life.
After tonight, nobody would want to direct or appear in the play adaptation of Agatha Christie's '*N or M'* ever again.
Her mother would be so proud of her.

*

David Wisbech conjured in his mind an image of the man that Agatha had warned him about. A Roman-nosed, light-skinned, dark-haired American. She had tried hard to convince him that the man might very well be related to Lanfranco Cassetti.

*

Judging by his apparent age and appearance, she thought the man she had encountered at *The Getaway Hotel* might be a son.

What harm could a man with ***any*** nose, let alone a ***Roman*** nose, do to interrupt this evening's performance?

It had been many years since David had taken on a role on stage other than as a stand-in for a sick actor but he had been rigorous in practicing his lines in '*N*'.

It was all part of a crazy plan cooked up by Agatha Christie and Arthur Hambleton.

He prayed earnestly that Peter Starling, playing Tommy Beresford, wouldn't shoot him dead! He didn't want to suffer the same dreadful fate as Duncan Morgan.

The ice cream lady lifted a small tub of vanilla from her tray and handed it to the man in a blue shirt and black tie.

"Thanks, honey," he said. "Will this cover it?"

He handed her a five pound note.

"If there's any change, keep it."

He strolled from the foyer into a corridor. The walls either side were lined with framed photographs of actors and actresses, past and present, alongside patrons and benefactors. Old black and white prints depicted the theatre's development over the years.

There would be a few more photos to add soon but they might not be helpful in attracting new patrons.

*

Holly Hollings' photo was one of those lining the corridor. Luigi thought she had a sweet smile.

She probably had a kind heart, too.

Shame it would stop beating in an hour or two.

It was just her bad luck to be appearing as Tuppence Beresford in tonight's performance.

It had been still worse luck that she had once played the death-dealing Mrs Hubbard in *'Murder on the Orient Express'*.

Mrs Hubbard, who had been in the compartment next to his father's. Mrs Hubbard who had been one of his murderers.

Several seats were already occupied although the performance was not due to start for another fifty minutes.

Somebody had carried through a steaming carton of coffee and another was reading a newspaper.

A woman of indeterminate age had settled into a seat in the centre of the second row. A large black handbag sat on the floor between her feet. She was wearing a coat with a brooch on its left lapel and a flat, somewhat old-fashioned hat. Pendent about her neck was a string of white pearls.

She was being observed.

Luigi Cassetti was amused by the way some older women hung on to their old familiar clothing for as long as they did.

The woman in the second row, for example. She had on a coat of a style not seen in his hometown of Chicago for umpteen years and an unfashionable hat that would attract sniggers if seen by any of the women in his circle of acquaintances.

He had a seat in the front row, thankfully, so wouldn't be distracted by those seated behind him.

He had noted the illuminated EMERGENCY EXIT sign directly to his left.

*

Out in the street, out of sight of theatregoers, two unmarked police vans had drawn up outside the door of theatre's emergency exit. Seated closely together inside each were two rows of lightly-armed police officers.

Arthur Hambleton, Chief Constable, Bournemouth district, did not **expect** trouble but he thought it wise to **anticipate** it.

The audience began drifting towards the theatre. Some hovered by the entrance and waited for friends to arrive. Others headed to the Box Office hoping that tickets might still be available for that evening's performance. A few walked straight in and climbed a flight of stairs to the upstairs cafeteria.

*

Aneka Baltz felt almost as excited as she felt nervous. She had hired a car for twenty-four hours. Her suitcase, packed and labelled, was in its boot. A passport, a one-way ferry ticket and currency were safely stored in a shoulder bag and easily to-hand.
That left plenty of time to drive the two hundred miles to Harwich. From there, the ferry would carry her to the Hook of Holland where her mother would be waiting. Together, they would make the journey by car to their home in Cuxhaven, Germany.
Before any of that could happen, though, she would need to curb her impatience. In an hour or so she would have a lasting memory to take away with her.

*

The chatter from the rows behind him was like the whispering of ghosts.

Luigi began to count in his head the number of actresses that had died at his hands.

There had been Mrs Hubbard, the grandmother of Daisy Armstrong. It had taken a single blow to the heart.

This was soon followed by his revenge attack on the actress playing Mary Debenham, Daisy's governess. The woman had put up a brave fight. He had been forced to slash her neck before driving the knife home through her heart.

According to his father, Princess Dragomiroff had been a loathsome creature, a woman who lied and was not to be trusted. Nobody need fear her words again.

Following the blow to her heart he had cut out her tongue.

Luigi sighed. His victims had been no more than actresses but they had readily adopted the roles of those women who had murdered his father.

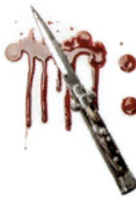

The theatre began to fill more rapidly as the minutes ticked by.

The curtain was due to rise in twenty minutes.

Backstage there were the usual moments of panic as performers forgot their lines, the lighting needed altering or somebody had tripped on a rope dangling from the gantry.

The make-up rooms began to empty and the performers made their way to the alcove where their stage props were stored.

Before long, an old-fashioned black telephone had been removed together with a wooden pipe, a green beret and a notebook.

The gun was pocketed.

The attendants closed the theatre doors. The audience settled in their seats. The lights dimmed.

'It was the spring of 1940. Tommy Beresford made sure he

was smiling as he walked into the sitting room where his wife sat knitting...'

The voice through the auditorium speakers sounded crisp and precise.

Mrs Beresford looked up at him.

"Anything interesting in the evening newspaper?"' she asked.

"Things look bad in France,'" Tommy said.

The first lines of *'M or N'* had been exchanged and Holly relaxed.

She was always afraid of forgetting her opening words and having to blunder on in a state of continual anxiety.

The more knowledgeable within the audience knew the origin of the play's title.

It had originated from the Latin, *'nomen vel nomina'* meaning *'name or names'*. It was an accident of typography that *'nomina'* came to be represented by *'m'*.

David Wisbech was possibly the most nervous of all the performers that evening. It had been the best part of two years since he had last set foot on stage as a performer. At least, as theatre director, he could easily correct any mistake in the following show. However, as a performer engaged in a live performance it was an option not available to him.

Holly Hollings almost always felt intoxicated by the atmosphere in a packed theatre. There was an air of expectancy which flowed between the auditorium and the stage. She truly wanted to create an agreeable impression in the mind of her friend, Agatha.

*

Holly glanced out at the audience during a short break between the first and second scenes. She spotted Agatha in the centre of the second row half-hidden behind a gentleman sitting directly in front of her. She noticed his fine Roman nose.

Aneka Baltz glanced impatiently at her watch. The scene she was hanging about for was not for another fifty minutes or so. It came immediately after the start of the second half. Perhaps it would have been wiser, she thought, to have simply got in the car and driven away whilst the coast was clear. There was another coast she needed to reach. The British coast at Harwich.

The desire to stay and watch her final act of retribution unfold was too great.

*

David Wisbech mused on the appearance of a Roman nose. He must have seen many in his lifetime but ask him to sketch one and he'd be flummoxed.

He stood stage right and awaited his cue.

While he marked time he cast a quick eye over the audience closest to him. The seats in the front rows were filled, all eyes pinned to the events unfolding on stage. There was no mistaking Agatha. Her clothing and tightly-curled fair hair was as distinctive and as unique as her books.

His view of her was partially obstructed by a gentleman in the centre of the front row. A tight smile played about his lips but he appeared - in that brief moment – to be nervous, his eyes darting back and forth between the characters on stage.

David thought the man's nose might be considered Roman.

*

The curtains swished across the stage as the first half of the play concluded. The audience applauded enthusiastically. Many rose from their seats and began their battle to the bar and the cafeteria during the twenty-minute interval. Agatha settled for a tub of strawberry ice cream from a young man with a tray hanging from his shoulders and then returned to her seat. She was forming ideas for her next book. She rather fancied calling it *'Stage Fright'*.

*

The curtains opened and a hush fell upon the audience. Agatha couldn't help but smile.

She knew what was about to happen.

Most of the audience did not.

The on-stage lighting had been dimmed which left the cellar in darkness. A feeble lightbulb was the only source of illumination.

Two figures stood in the shadow cast by the meagre shafts of light.

Agatha knew what was about to happen. She'd written the book!

*

The audience gave vent to a collective gasp.

Leaning against the far wall of the cellar stood a figure that several members of the audience recognised immediately. It was David Wisbech, director of *The Bournemouth Arts Theatre.*

On this occasion, however, he was dressed in a tweed sports jacket, corduroy trousers and brown leather shoes. *On this occasion* he was dressed in Commander Haydock's favourite clothes.

Beneath his expensive country attire his heart was pounding.

Standing in the entrance to the cellar, Tommy Beresford extended his arm and aimed the pistol directly at

Commander Haydock.

"**Let her go**!" he yelled. "Let her go and I won't hurt you."

"Why don't I believe you?" mocked Haydock.

Tuppence Beresford choked as Haydock's left arm gripped her throat more tightly.

"We've discovered what you've been up to behind the façade of respectability you present to your aristocratic friends."

"You're a spy! You've been working for Nazi Germany," Tommy said.

Haydock sneered.

"Clever you, Mister Beresford. You're quite right."

Tommy watched as his wife, Tuppence, struggled to draw breath.

"Perhaps we could work out a deal?" he suggested frantically, desperation clear in his voice.

"I'd rather die than deal! But I won't die alone," Commander Haydock retorted.

He reached into his right-hand jacket pocket and withdrew a small handgun. He raised it to Tuppence's head but she twisted her body to one side just as his finger pulled on the trigger.

There was an explosion.

The audience gasped in horror just as Agatha had predicted.

The sound of the explosion ricocheted off the theatre walls.

Commander Haydock, the German spy nicknamed '*N*', lay sprawled on the floor. Blood spilled from his chest onto the floor around him.

A droll thought entered his head as he lay prone in a red sea of gore.

Water and a soft brush would quickly remove the burgundy-coloured fluid from the transparent plastic sheet on which he lay and it would be ready for tomorrow afternoon's matinee.

*

David Wisbech continued to lay prone on the stage.

He knew what had happened and he felt like screaming.

The tension inside of him felt as explosive as the bullet lying beside him.

It had been for real. Somebody had tried to murder him! The atmosphere in the theatre had turned ghostlike in its silence as the curtains closed on Act Two.

*

David rose to his feet.
The full-body protective shield provided by Chief Constable Arthur Hambleton had probably saved his life. The actor who had portrayed Tommy Beresford was distraught.
"My God!" he mumbled haltingly. "I thought I'd killed him."
David Wisbech was no less distressed.
"That gun had blanks in it last night. Arthur Hambleton and I checked it ourselves."

*

The deafening explosion could be heard clearly from as far away as the foyer where Aneka stood pretending to read posters for forthcoming productions.

She walked casually out of the theatre and on to the pavement.

Aneka expressed no surprise or reaction as, from the corners of her eyes, she took in the two unmarked police vehicles.

She was an actress and a good one at that. A master of disguise...or should that be a *mistress* of disguise in this politically-correct age?

The police ignored the bearded man in dirty denim jeans and a filthy sweatshirt that shuffled past their waiting vans. The scruffily-dressed figure took a left turn fifty yards later and stopped beside an old red Mazda 3 parked within the white boundary lines of a long-term parking bay.

Within thirty seconds the vehicle's engine was running and the jeans and sweatshirt lay in the well of the car. As it moved away, Aneka grinned. She'd forgotten to remove the beard.

Vengeance delivered. Mission achieved.

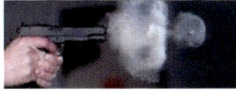

When the curtains reopened to reveal the scene for the start of the final act the audience had settled back down. Tuppence Beresford was being held tightly in her husband's arms.

"I thought I was going to lose you," he murmured as he stroked her hair.

"It was only your quick thinking that saved me," Tuppence replied.

"Not at all. If you hadn't twisted away from Commander Haydock at the last moment, as you did, then I would have been *his* target...and an easy one at that!"

"But I'm quite safe now that I'm in your arms," she smiled.

*

Luigi Cassetti took another glance towards the emergency exit door to the left of where he was seated.

The action was now moving rapidly between the right and left hand sides of the stage. He sneaked a look at his watch. There wasn't a great deal of time remaining. He needed to act very soon or it would be too late.

107

An image drifted into his mind. It was of an old black and white photograph his mother had taken of him and his father in the backyard of their Chicago home. He was just sixteen at the time but had already been taught how to survive and prosper in the corrupt world of his father's nefarious businesses. His father's arm was around his shoulder and he had whispered some words in his ear just before the click of the Kodak's shutter.

"You're the son of Lanfranco Cassetti. Honour your family. Be loyal to your friends. Destroy your enemies."

Luigi was still the son of Lanfranco Cassetti. He still honoured his family and was still loyal to his friends. Now it was time to destroy another enemy just as that enemy had destroyed his father.

Holly had known it might be dangerous embracing an opportunity to play Tuppence Beresford in *'M or 'N'*. After all, some had even *lost their lives* in the role. She realised she was acting as bait for the person responsible for their murders.

Agatha's eyes followed Holly as she moved towards the centre of the stage.

Agatha coughed twice, somewhat loudly. This was the pre-arranged signal.

Several members of the audience in the front-rows turned towards her in annoyance.

Holly raised a hand and touched her nose. This was the pre-arranged acknowledgement. Holly dropped to her knees and then lay flat on the floor.

The audience gasped as a piercing shriek rent the air.

Luigi Cassetti was on his feet. His right arm was drawn back and in his hand he held a stiletto knife with a long slender blade and needle-like point.

The knife was about to begin its lethal journey.

Luigi screamed.

He dropped the knife and clutched the back of his neck.

Impaled in it was Agatha's hatpin.

Luigi tugged the hatpin free, leapt to his feet and dashed to the emergency exit door to his left.

He tugged on the bar but it didn't budge.

The audience screamed as armed police advanced cautiously down the side and centre aisles.

"Everybody! Keep your heads down!"

It was the voice of Chief Constable Arthur Hambleton.

Luigi levered himself up on to the stage.

He walked towards its centre and sneered at the figure of Holly Hollings who still lay prone on the floor.

"Murderer!" he yelled.

Holly lifted her eyes in surprise.

"Caroline Hubbard! You murdered my father. You and the rest of your gang of murderers."

He slid a gun out from beneath the belt of his trousers.

The audience cried out in panic.

He raised the gun and began pulling its trigger.

Agatha smashed her handbag hard against the back of his head and he stumbled. She had managed to scramble up the steps and on to the stage.

"For you, my dear."

Luigi was thrown off-balance.

The bullet penetrated the wooden trap door and lodged in electrical cables running beneath the stage.

The theatre lighting failed and the auditorium turned

black.

After two minutes, emergency lighting lit the theatre in a dim glow.

Luigi Cassetti was not to be seen.

The emergency doors on either side of the front row hung open. Staff had unlocked them by torchlight shortly after the theatre had been plunged into darkness to allow the audience to escape.

The first person to avail himself of the opportunity had been Luigi Cassetti.

It had been an astonishing year for *The Bournemouth Arts Theatre* and its Director, David Wisbech.

Duncan Morgan had been murdered on stage in *'M or N'* after the dummy gun intended for use in the production had been switched with another containing live ammunition.

Indeed, it had been bizarre for the town itself and alarming for its residents. There had been a series of murders with no obvious connection other than that the victims had all been female actresses. By coincidence, or maybe not, they had all appeared in *'Murder on The Orient Express.'*

Agatha Christie had offered a theory that was rejected on the grounds of mere speculation.

She had suggested that a fellow guest at *The Welcome Hotel* had been related to Lanfranco Cassetti, the gangster stabbed to death aboard that infamous train.

She suggested, too, that Hilary Williams was actually Aneka Baltz, the daughter of Monika Baltz, the German spy.

In her opinion both her suspects were seeking revenge on behalf of their parents.

She was told her theories were the stuff of books to which she had replied, rather tartly,

"Yes, my dear, I know. I wrote the books!"

*

Monika Baltz hugged her daughter and promised them both a holiday.
"*Not in Britain!*" her mother teased. "*Italy, perhaps.*"
"*Or maybe Chicago?*" Aneka suggested. "*I've heard it's an exciting city.*"

*

Luigi Cassetti was surprised at the ease with which he was able to return to Chicago. Of course, the fake passport and papers helped together with a few subtle alterations to his appearance.
His flight had landed in New York where a white Mercedes was waiting to drive him to Chicago.

*

It was December in Britain and up and down the country Christmas pantomimes were in full swing.

113

Holly Hollings was a very happy young lady.
Christmas pantomimes were in full swing and she had a
starring role as *Alice* in *'Alice in Wonderland.'*

There were sprigs of holly decorating the dining table in
her parent's home.

It was Christmas Day and her birthday.
David Wisbech was holding her left hand.
There was an engagement ring on its third finger.

Next Spring, they would be married and rehearsals for
their next production would begin. Holly looked forward
to her role as Lorna Keating in *'The Hangman's Noose'*.

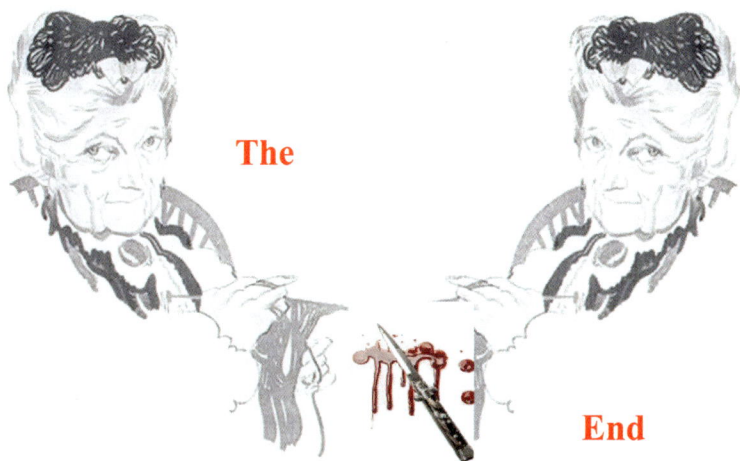

The

End

On the following pages…

'THE LITTLE BEDROOM'
A short story from the book
'A TWIST IN THE TAIL'

THE LITTLE BEDROOM (Story 14)

I put the onions on top of the rest of the groceries and trudged home wearily. The rain was falling in a fine mist. The sky was dark and heavy with cloud and Simon was leaving home. It was a grey day in more ways than one.

It seemed only yesterday that I was the centre of his universe but today he was eighteen and his guitar and an old Ford Escort were more meaningful.

We chose the wallpaper for his bedroom together. Six rolls were more than enough and I still had one spare in the loft. But Simon was a thoughtful boy who loved and cared for his little den and the extra roll was never needed.

The world is larger than ten feet by ten and Simon wanted to explore it. It was partly Jim's fault. He'd sneaked away from home to go to sea when he was barely sixteen. He lied about his age and the captain didn't ask too many questions. Don't get me wrong, though. Jim's a wonderful husband and he's been a fine father to Simon. I just wish he hadn't made his bedtime stories sound quite so sparkling.

A car splashed me as it passed through a pool of water on the road. I'd have to wash the mud off my stockings when I reached home. I didn't really want to go home. I didn't want to return to an empty house.

It was my idea so I shouldn't really grumble. But it couldn't stop the words spinning round inside my head.

"I don't know how to say good-bye," said Simon.

"You go while I'm out shopping," I replied. "It'll be easier."

In a way, of course, it *was* easier. No tears, no last minute recriminations. Unshared, they would come later when I was alone. Jim didn't like emotional scenes. I don't blame him. It's just his way.

"The lad'll be fine," Jim had said. "He's a man now. He's eighteen."

I crossed the road and turned into Freeman's Avenue. Simon was a still a boy in my eyes. Eighteen was a number. It didn't make him a man.

"Hello, Mrs Warner. Isn't it today that Simon's moving into his new bedsit?"

I turned around. She must have come out of the post office.

"That's right," I said to my neighbour.

Perhaps I looked glum. Perhaps she noticed a tear glisten

in the corner of one eye.

"You've got to let him go *sometime*," she said gently.

"I'm proud of him. I'm pleased that he wants to stand on

his own two feet," I replied unconvincingly.

"Don't dwell on it," she advised. "He's eighteen, isn't he?

If he's old enough to vote, he's old enough to leave

home."

I'd been old enough to vote twenty years ago when you

had to be twenty one but I hadn't felt the need to leave

home. It was Jim who finally persuaded me. I can't really

blame him, though. He never really enjoyed living with

my parents.

The rain was easing slightly and there were blue cracks in

the sky.

I had a lot to do when I got home.

Nowadays, twenty years was a long time to stay married

and Jim and I had earned ourselves a small celebration. A

few glasses of sweet sherry would bring back a few

memories.

I remember feeling slightly disappointed when Simon was

born. I'd have liked a girl but I was happy for Jim. He

wanted a boy. You couldn't really blame him for that,

could you, and Simon *was* a beautiful baby.

I remember pushing an enormous pram around the park

for hours on end while Jim was at work in the cotton

factory. Simon was a weepy baby and my feet used to

ache by the time I'd trundled him to sleep.

I remember Jim playing football with him in the back yard

and then a few years later they were off to football

matches on a Saturday. It was only right that I should stay

home. After all, they were hungry when they came back

and it was only proper to have a hot meal waiting for

them. I didn't like football much, anyway.

I didn't care much for fishing, either. On a Sunday, when they were out sitting along by the river, I had a chance to tidy the house. I used to spend more time then was necessary in Simon's bedroom. It was hard to accept that the little room had been home to a baby, a boy and now, everyone seemed to be saying, a man.

I opened the wooden gate. I must get Jim to put another coat of creosote on it before the autumn sets in.

The house was quiet. I put down the shopping and switched on the radio. *The Archers* would be on in a moment or two. It was comforting to know that some things were constant in life.

I wondered what Simon would have forgotten to take with him. It would be nice to visit him in his new bedsit. I didn't imagine for one moment that he would be there on his own but I didn't want to pry. I just hoped she would look after him and, who knows, they might stay together for a long time. For twenty years, perhaps, although these days...

I didn't care to think how many thousand times I had plodded up these stairs. Eighteen years ago I carried nappies. Today I had Jim's best white going-out shirt draped over my arm. It had dried well in front of the fire.

I hesitated as I walked past Simon's door. Something made me turn back. I think I needed to have a final look around the room before Jim came home for lunch. Or, perhaps, I needed something to remind me that Simon hadn't wiped me from his memory so soon. After all, he'd forgotten to leave me a note downstairs. I didn't even have his new address.

I pushed open the door. It creaked nervously, just as it had done for years. I must ask Jim to put some oil on the hinges.

"Simon!" I exclaimed.

"Hi, mum. Surprised to see me, huh?"

He must have anticipated my astonishment and yet he

looked so calm and composed.

"I changed my mind," he said. "I don't think I'm quite

ready to leave home. I'm only eighteen, after all."

"But your friend ...?" I began and immediately felt guilty

at the insinuation.

"What friend's that, mum?" he asked disconsolately.

I caught sight of the letter on his bed. It was torn in two.

Beside it lay a crumpled envelope.

When he looked up at me his eyes sparkled. Tears can do

that.

"I'll tell your dad they let the bedsit to someone else," I whispered.

"Would you, mum?" His face brightened. "It's just that dad'll feel I've failed him."

Twenty years of marriage flashed past in an instant.

"You haven't failed *me*, Simon," I said kindly. " I'm pleased you're still here."

"Families *should* stay together, shouldn't they, mum?" he asked bravely.

"Until they're ready to go," I replied softly.

I turned back at the door.

"Don't forget to come down for a glass of sherry this evening."

He smiled and I added, "You and your father are good together."

I took a final glance round the little bedroom and then did something I've never done before. I winked at Simon.

END

Printed in Poland
by Amazon Fulfillment
Poland Sp. z o.o., Wrocław